WHO CAN FIX IT?

written & illustrated by
Leslie Ann MacKeen

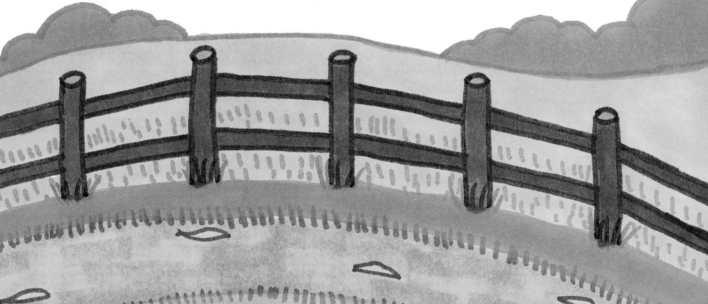

LANDMARK EDITIONS, INC.
P.O. Box 4469 • 1420 Kansas Avenue • Kansas City, Missouri 64127
(816) 241-4919

Dedicated to

my family and friends
who helped make this book
a special experience for me.

Second Printing

COPYRIGHT © 1989 BY LESLIE ANN MacKEEN

International Standard Book Number: 0-933849-19-2 (LIB.BDG.)

Library of Congress Cataloging-in-Publication Data
MacKeen, Leslie Ann, 1978-
   Who can fix it?
   Summary: When Jeremiah's car breaks down on the way to his mother's house,
several animals stop by to offer amusing solutions to his problem.
   [1. Automobiles — Maintenance and repair — Fiction.
   2. Animals — Fiction.   3.Children's writings.]
I. Title.
PZ7.M19449Wh   1989   [E] — dc19   89-31819

Editorial Coordinator: Nancy R. Thatch
Creative Coordinator: David Melton

Printed in the United States of America

Landmark Editions, Inc.
P.O. Box 4469
1420 Kansas Avenue
Kansas City, Missouri 64127
(816) 241-4919

WHO CAN FIX IT?

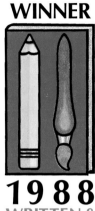

In the course of the last twelve years, I have had the privilege of working with thousands of students of all ages in Written & Illustrated by... Workshops throughout the United States.

I am continually fascinated by the students' individual approaches to writing and illustrating their original books. Some students work analytically, others intuitively. Some work slowly, while others attack the pages with the speed of summer lightning.

Leslie Ann MacKeen definitely uses the "summer lightning" approach. I can't recall having ever seen anyone work faster or more decisively than Leslie. And I have never worked with a more congenial young lady. She listens carefully to suggestions, then immediately begins to synthesize ideas. In short, Leslie Ann is a whiz!

While the winning students and their parents are at Landmark, the students spend considerable periods of time working in the private office we provide for them. Not so with Leslie Ann. She would take an hour's worth of work into her office, and in only twenty minutes, she'd be back in my office with a finished illustration, ready to start something new. However, her "summer lightning" speed was no problem. Instead, it posed a delightful full-time challenge for me and our staff.

When Leslie Ann returned to her home in Winston-Salem, North Carolina, I wasn't surprised that within days we began to receive some finished illustrations. And I wasn't at all surprised when the rest of her illustrations were completed well ahead of deadlines.

As Leslie Ann created the misadventures of Jeremiah T. Fitz, it was fun to watch her develop her book and to see the delightful whimsy and gentle humor displayed in her work. I invite you to now enjoy her wonderful book.

— David Melton
Creative Coordinator
Landmark Editions, Inc.

Every Sunday afternoon,
Jeremiah T. Fitz had dinner with his mother.

One Sunday, as he drove along the country road
to her house, his car quit running and rolled to a stop.
He knew the car could not be out of gas
because he had filled the tank that very morning.

6

Jeremiah T. Fitz got out of the car,
and he turned the crank again and again.
But his car would not start.

"Who can fix it?" Jeremiah T. Fitz wondered aloud.

"You can fix it!" said Kara Kangaroo as she hopped
up the road. "All you have to do is give your car a jump start."

So Jeremiah T. Fitz pulled out the jumper cable,
and he jumped, and jumped, and jumped.
But his car would not start.

"Who can fix it?" asked Jeremiah.

"You can fix it!" said Elmo Elephant.
"Just look in the trunk. Maybe there's a peanut stuck in it."

So Jeremiah T. Fitz opened the trunk and looked inside.
He took out a jack, a spare tire, and an old pair of gloves.
But he didn't find any peanuts, and his car would not start.

"Who can fix it?" asked Jeremiah.

"You can fix it!" said Clyde Camel. "All you have to do is check the water. I always fill up before a trip."

So Jeremiah T. Fitz took off his shoe and his sock, and he dipped his toes into the radiator. There was more than enough water, but still his car would not start.

"Who can fix it?" asked Jeremiah.

"You can fix it!" said Gloria Gorilla. "All you have to do is
hang around until you think of something."

So Jeremiah T. Fitz grabbed hold of a tree limb.
He thought and he thought,
but he couldn't think of anything to do.
And his car would not start.

"Who can fix it?" asked Jeremiah.

"You can fix it!" hissed Simone Snake. "Your car may need more oil, so it can s-s-s-slither along."

So Jeremiah T. Fitz picked up Sylvester Snake,
straightened out his coils, and dipped him into the oil tank.
"No problem here," said Jeremiah. "There's plenty of oil."
But his car would not start.

"Who can fix it?" asked Jeremiah.

"You can fix it!" said Petunia Peacock. "All you have to do is check the fan belt."

So Jeremiah T. Fitz took off his belt, and he fanned and fanned. But his car would not start.

"Who can fix it?" asked Jeremiah.

"You can fix it!" said Flora, Floyd and Fanny Firefly as they flitted about. "Just check the spark plugs."

So Jeremiah T. Fitz opened the hood.
And when he took hold of the spark plugs,
he got the shock of his life. Still his car would not start.

"Who can fix it?" asked Jeremiah.

"You can fix it!" said Barnabus Bear. "All you have to do is scare the problem out of your car."

So Jeremiah T. Fitz made a scary face, and he growled
his loudest, most ferocious growl.
But his car would not start.

"Who can fix it?" asked Jeremiah.

"I can fix it!" said Samantha Spider as she crawled
from beneath the hood. "This is mine," she said, pulling out
a web she had spun the night before. "It got stuck in the motor.
Now your car will start."

24

Sure enough, when Jeremiah T. Fitz turned the crank,
the motor sputtered three times, and then it started with a roar.

Jeremiah was so happy.

He thanked all his animal friends for their help
and invited them to dinner.

And when Jeremiah and his friends arrived
at his mother's house for dinner . . .
Boy, was she surprised!